Jolly Old Santa Claus

Jolly Old Santa Claus

Written by
Maryjane Hooper Tonn

Illustrated by
George Hinke

ideals children's books.
Nashville, Tennessee

ISBN-13: 978-0-8249-5626-4

Published by Ideals Children's Books
An imprint of Ideals Publications
A Guideposts Company
Nashville, Tennessee
www.idealsbooks.com

Printed and bound in China

Library of Congress CIP data on file

Leo_Jul10_1

Designed by Marisa Jackson

"Ho, ho, ho!" chuckled Jolly Old Santa Claus as he stroked his long white beard and laughed.

Mrs. Santa Claus and all the little elves came over to see what Santa was laughing about.

"What is so funny?" they asked.

"This is a letter from a little boy," said Jolly Old Santa Claus. "Can you guess what he wants to know?"

The elves all tried to guess. "Will he get a train for Christmas? Will we find his new house?"

"No," chuckled Jolly Old Santa Claus. "This little boy wants to know if we are busy at the North Pole!"

"Are we busy!" shouted the elves. "We most certainly are!"

The North Pole is the busiest place in the world just before Christmas. Come with me, and we'll visit the North Pole.

Then you can see for yourself what is happening there.

Let's first stop at the cookie kitchen. Look at the elves scurrying about with smudges of flour on their aprons. How hard they are working!

Oops, Grampa Elf fell. The big sack of flour is heavy, and he was walking backwards into the kitchen.

There's Jingles sitting on top of the oven and telling the elves how to place the trays of cookies so they won't burn.

Aren't you glad when Christmas comes and you can eat cookies?

But we must hurry on. There is much to see.

Here is the candy kitchen!
Santa and the elves are making
candy canes, lollipops,
peppermint drops, and cotton
candy. Look at the elves pouring
milk into the pot for fudge.
Uh-oh, one little elf has tripped
over Santa's cat, Lady Whiskers,
and spilled the frosted
brownies.

Santa and the elves are making
a lot of candy to fill the stockings
of good little boys and girls.

Now let's go to the toy shop,
where wonderful toys are made.

Isn't this a wonderful place? Everyone is busy, except for Lazy Elf. He's riding the rock-a-bye pony when he should be working.

Jolly Old Santa Claus is checking his list of toys: airplanes, trains, drums, blocks, dolls, teddy bears, and bouncing balls.

There are so many toys to finish before Christmas. Do you see Lady Whiskers? She is Santa's favorite cat. Do you see Merry One falling down the stairs? I think the jack-in-the-box frightened him.

Look at the clock on the wall. It's getting late, and Christmas will soon be here.

While the elves in the toy shop finish the toys, let's see about the Christmas trees.

Christmas trees grow all over the forest.

Look at the little animals in the forest. They love to watch the elves collecting the trees.

Do you see Grampa Elf? He's slipped in the snow and lost his cap! He's the funniest elf, isn't he? And he never remembers to wear his glasses.

Do you see Lazy Elf? I wonder where he is. He's probably out talking to the reindeer.

Now, let's go to the ornament room.

Isn't this a beautiful room! There are so many bright colors and pretty ornaments for the Christmas trees. Look—in the corner, the elves are blowing glass ornaments.

This is a special job, and only the most careful elves can work here. The glass ornaments must be handled very carefully or they will break.

Do you see Lady Whiskers? She's high in the rafters watching. If she walked on the floor, her tail would break the ornaments. Chief Elf wouldn't like that at all.

And there's Bashful Elf, sitting on top of the tool shelf so no one can see him.

Here is Mrs. Claus in front of Santa's castle. She is making sure that everything will be ready for Santa to leave on time. He must not be late!

The elves are putting toys into the sleigh. Look at that teddy bear. He's so big that two elves have to carry him.

Chief Elf has Santa's route in his hand and knows just where the reindeer must stop.

Jingles is leading the reindeer out to hook them up to the sleigh.

What does Mrs. Santa Claus have in her hands? Are those earmuffs and a heavy scarf to keep Santa Claus warm on his long trip tonight?

For tonight is the night. At long last it is here. It is the night before Christmas.

The stars are twinkling in the sky. All the world is hushed and still, waiting for this magical night.

For tonight—yes, tonight—he comes. Swiftly through the skies they will fly—Jolly Old Santa Claus and his eight reindeer.

And more quietly than softly falling snow, he will land atop your house.

And then, silently—oh, so silently—he will put a pack of toys on his back and slide down your chimney.

Santa will fill your stocking with goodies and place wonderful surprises beneath your tree.

Who knows what dear old Santa Claus will leave? But he is sure to have read your letter before the elves packed up the toys for his journey.

Then, just as quietly and just as quickly as he came, in the wink of an eye, he will be gone.

Santa will spring up the chimney and back to his sleigh and his faithful reindeer. And all through the night they will fly. They will crisscross the world, bringing happiness and joy and love into the homes of all little children.

And long before the sun rises in the Christmas morning sky, Jolly Old Santa Claus will have visited the homes of every good little boy and girl all over the world. Then he will fly back to his home at the North Pole.

And there will be such excitement when he returns home!

The little elves will want to know all about Jolly Old Santa Claus's trip.

"Did it snow, Santa?"

"Was it very cold?"

"Were the little boys and girls asleep in their beds?"

But look at Lady Whiskers! She has a surprise for Santa. She's brought him four soft, cuddly little kittens.

While the elves feed the reindeer and settle them down, Jolly Old Santa Claus will tell them all about his trip.

Here comes Mrs. Santa Claus. She has made hot chocolate and cookies for Santa!

He is very tired and very hungry after his long night's journey.

Now the elves are all very busy, including Kindly Elf, who is shining Santa's boots and polishing the bells from his sleigh.

Santa's helpers are unpacking the unused toys very carefully so they can be used next year.

Look at Impy Elf spilling the bucket of red paint! He's so excited to have Santa back from his trip.

Soon all of the work will be finished. Then Jolly Old Santa Claus and Mrs. Santa Claus and the elves will be ready to rest.

But before they go to bed, Mrs. Claus will sit down at the organ while the elves pump the foot pedal. Music will fill the air, and Jolly Old Santa Claus will sing out:

Silent night! Holy night!
All is calm, all is bright
Round yon virgin, mother and child.
Holy infant, so tender and mild,
Sleep in heavenly peace.
Sleep in heavenly peace.

As the sun comes over the North Pole, Jolly Old Santa Claus,

Mrs. Claus, and all of the elves will say "Merry Christmas"

to one another. Then Jolly Old Santa Claus will call out,

"Merry Christmas to all boys
and girls around the world."